Hold Still Fast

Sean Pravica

Hold Still Fast by Sean Pravica

ISBN: 978-1-949790-32-0

eISBN: 978-1-949790-33-7

Copyright © 2020 Sean Pravica

Layout and book design by Mark Givens

Front cover photograph by Sean Pravica

Author photo by Danelze Strydom

First Pelekinesis Printing 2020

For information: Pelekinesis, 112 Harvard Ave #65, Claremont, CA 91711 USA

Library of Congress Cataloging-in-Publication Data

Names: Pravica, Sean, 1984- author.
Title: Hold still fast / Sean Pravica.
Description: Claremont, CA : Pelekinesis, [2020]
Identifiers: LCCN 2019048727 (print) | LCCN 2019048728 (ebook) | ISBN 9781949790320 (paperback) | ISBN 9781949790337 (epub)
Subjects: LCSH: Characters and characteristics--Fiction. | Perception--Fiction. | Flash fiction, American. | Short stories, American. | Psychological fiction.
Classification: LCC PS3616.R387 .A6 2020 (print) | LCC PS3616.R387 (ebook) | DDC 813/.6--dc23
LC record available at https://lccn.loc.gov/2019048727
LC ebook record available at https://lccn.loc.gov/2019048728

Hold Still Fast

by

Sean Pravica

For Danelze, for whom two words are perfect:

Boom boom.

CONTENTS

HOLD STILL FAST

Her eyes were still wet going in. The elevator was a tube fixed to the outside of the building, so that the city shot towards your face if you pressed it against the glass and looked down. We kissed instead, missed nothing and everything, our hot-tongued protest against time.

SAME DIFFERENCE

They read together with their feet in the creek water. It was a dry heat day. Little flying things drifted slowly around them, the air breathing quiet, soft and humming.

They covered many pages, then talked about what happened. Their interpretations worlds apart, though their passage the same.

INTERPRETATIVE DANCE

It was Opening Night, the audience silent. Their attention, their engagement, a buzzing wire upon which the actors danced, never fluttering towards the void. The director swelled.

But then came laughter, and then more, until it roared. A standing ovation. The director, her cast, searching. A mutual loss of understanding.

PLAY

She played guitar on the city street. Her red hair dripped over her shoulders like melted wax. Ratty and knotted, wooden beads enclosed in its dready parts like pearls in clam shells.

Someone dropped a crumpled dollar bill, her guitar case closed. It almost stopped her, but she played on.

GRIN AND BEAR IT

The speaker spoke about happiness in the workplace. It was a required seminar for the employees.

He wore a yellow shirt. Had years working to support his thesis. Had years of jokes, anecdotes.

He appeared reasonably happy, more than they did, sitting, listening, stapled packets about positive thinking beside them.

HOW ARE YOU?

The short-order cook stepped out from behind the counter to say hello to her. He had not seen her in years. His shift had just ended. Perfect timing.

"Good to see you!"

"You too!"

She asked him many questions about his brother and sister, their careers and families.

LIKE A BANANA PEEL

Synthetic music blared from horn-shaped speakers at the car wash. The sign was a painted clown's face, its smile a red and white grid, eyes little blue dots. The workers were efficient, their uniforms wet with grime. One slipped on a rag. A customer laughed. No one else noticed.

INVENTORY

He painted intersecting lines and shapes.

Acrylics. Oils. Broad strokes. Many colors.

Many colors.

His paintings did not sell. Not much anyway. Or for much, either.

Sometimes a coffee shop hung them. Mostly, he stored them in crates in his closet.

Well, lately they were spilling into his bedroom.

HOME FOR THE HOLIDAYS

He rolled in with his oxygen tank, greeting others buoyantly. He was dressed in a wet suit and wore flippers on his feet, which had not supported his weight in years.

"Your grandpa is dressed like a scuba diver! Dude that's awesome."

"He makes the most of it."

CAFE OFF THE
INTERSTATE

She poured coffee for the millionth customer she called "Hun." She sang along, 1950's stuff, moving behind the stainless steel countertop with speed and life. She had worked there for many years.

No one knew what it took her to get there. Only that she was the best.

ABOUT US

She was an empath. A sponge to the room's moods.

She hated his boss after the story he told, and not that the story told much. He seethed.

She cried that her dog ran away. Where could it have gone?

She only asked questions. The room's most interesting person.

AUDIENCE

"I wrote a poem. Want to hear it?"

"Is it about me?"

"No."

A pause.

"How long is it?"

.

MUSE

She enjoyed driving—time to think, to look. Really *hear* music.

For the experience, she picked up a hitchhiker. He was also a musician.

He used to write jingles but jobs ran dry.

She dropped him off where he asked, at a hostel.

She wrote a song about it.

THE SLIP

He didn't need them. He was making music. Par-adiddling the kitchen counter snare, hammering the linoleum bass.

He shut the lights off for a flashlight strobe show.

All alone. All his. He didn't need anyone. He didn't need anyone ever again.

PLAY DATE

The electricity was off again. The boy's friend spent the night. Flashlights and stories. Cold pop tarts.

In the morning, already beating hot, they ran through the sprinklers on dirt and brown grass. She watched from the kitchen window, listening to laughter. When the boy looked up she turned away.

REMEMBER WHEN

He heard her laughing from the other room. It carried like a siren on another street, a world apart but demanding attention.

He walked to the doorway but stopped short, listened to the rich joy of her unburdened voice.

Who did it?

How?

She stopped when she saw him.

SPA DAY

The bubbles foamed over the side of the tub. She used extra mix on purpose, listening to the soft, constant crackle from lively suds.

She was a little too relaxed, never heard the door open and suddenly they were home, shrieking. It was desperate, but she escaped out their window.

NEIGHBORHOOD WATCH

The ice water bath got easier. Somewhat. His pain was lessened afterwards, numbed. Loosened his broken fingers. As he called them, anyway.

The dog, limping, got its food.

Two old dogs, he would say.

Crosswords, solitaire. Long time looking out the window, the other old dog by his side.

THE SEER

He occupied a bench near the coffee shop where he spoke to himself in sweeping monologues.

"They said police did that. Police didn't do that. What happens to criminals? They get married!" he exclaimed, laughing knowingly, hands clapping.

He spoke in epiphanies. A hidden order in plain sight.

THE VISITOR

It was after midnight and he was still writing. Good stuff. Late night stories. The others fast asleep.

Someone knocked at the door.

He looked, skin pricked wide awake.

He stood, fist raised, a strange readiness.

A shape moved away outside the window.

He watched it disappear, return to silence.

PILLOW TALK

They fell asleep with the window left open, the peach drapes wind-whipped into playful undulations. He woke suddenly and rose to shut it, shivering. He turned and took two quick steps but something stopped him. She shifted, said that name again, her voice elongated in its distant, dreamy way.

HOUSEKEEPING

No one had made the bed in days, sheets strewn chaotically.

They were on the floor now, stoned and laughing, music blaring, abandoned finger-paintings in primary colors.

Their families did not know they were here. They would both go home tomorrow, and would make the bed before they left.

TIME MACHINE

She was in the hotel room smoking another cigarette. The world outside the window was obnoxious, demanding.

She used an ashtray, chipped brown plastic. It made everything feel dated. She liked it, wished the text messages she was reading were handwritten letters instead. Then she could burn them.

WELD

Sparks flew against the still, black night. A scrabble of scrap metal scattered in his orderless dirt yard.

He lived in what, before the fire, was a prosperous mining town. Few people or buildings remained. There were no schools, police, functioning businesses.

He had all he wanted, his secrets kept.

NIGHT DRIVE ALONG A DESERT HIGHWAY

The highway was a theatre to headlights and tail-lights. Also flashing radio towers, blinking blue-white in space, the outline of hills behind them endlessly black.

She wondered about the others. Who were they and where were they going?

Maybe they all wondered the same thing. Satellites beaming, signals silent.

PERFORMANCE

She played the clarinet, feet crossed and tucked under the stool. Leaning forward, shoulders raised, she was a fixed concentration of labor and memory. The perfect absence of everyone hummed with each note. A shaft of sunlight dropped through the auditorium window, itself a golden stage to dust motes dancing.

ALONE TIME TO ENJOY NATURE

He played his wooden flute in the desert, feet dangling off the rock he perched on, looking up at the birds soaring past him.

He punched high notes into the air, returning their call. He never consciously meant to fall, to fly with them. It was all just so beautiful.

RECORD STORE IN THE FUTURE

It was 10:00. Then 10:01. Still the doors locked. An employee stirred inside, signaling that opening was imminent.

Finally the guy waiting outside got his chance, after eagerly peeking through the windows while his legs shook with incessant jitters.

A lovely thing to see in 2020, whatever we are.

PROMISE

The death card shows up frequently in his tarot readings, which he receives monthly. Probably rears its boney head four times a year. Maybe more.

Of course it's actually a good card to draw. Change. Nothing more promising, really. The sun waits to crest, but the light is nigh.

DISCOVERY

They started before sunrise. This was the fastest they reached the water.

They saw the pale, tumid arm first, but did not recognize it. The rest—unblinking eyes, colorless lips—came clear as they got closer.

She held her quaking body, told her it was okay. A mantra on repeat.

SCRATCHED RECORD

The walls felt smaller while they shook. Frail pops. All else rattled, a nervous twitch.

It was over quickly and nothing was damaged. The epicenter just four something, and a city over. Enough only to say hello, to remind them what was possible.

Or at least to interrupt their fight.

SHELTER

It was summer. The school gymnasium was the most immediately available space large enough to fit the people. Many of them had children at the school. The building sweltered with their presence.

A volunteer rolled in a wheelbarrow full of watermelons. His picture made the front page of the paper.

HEART

A flash of light, a birth. Neon violet, rich blue. A faint orange ring lining the flame's heart.

She prolonged the match, digesting its simple utility, snuffing it when the heat burned too hot at her fingertips.

The power out for the fourth day, she looked more closely at things.

RELIVE

They drove together and talked about the past. Good stories only, lived again in their retelling.

Up the mountain, parked at a particular turnout, they made love. They clawed, groped, remembering one story with all their heart. Back then, it had no other stories to frame it, not like now.

PARLOR TRICKS

The game was to open up bottles of beer for ten different people using a different household object each time. He did so, in about five minutes.

Then, having a cigarette, he halved a wood plank with a causal heel kick.

Finally, he undid her bra strap. With her help.

FOR THE MILLIONTH TIME

The puckering reek of disinfectant wipes hovered as a specter of false sterility, unable to obscure the underlying sweat stink. Even the iron smelled, used and greasy. She loved it, these trenches of effort, time invested. He walked over, winked yet again. She dropped the weight. That look! That foot.

NO ONE GETS HURT

Snails crawled across palm fronds, over lines of yellow translucence. He picked them off, watched their vague bodies jerk back into their shells in sudden bursts of reflexive speed.

He tossed the shells over the fence to the open field next door. They would be back, but so would he.

ROLL AGAIN

A blue Monday night with plain-lighted kitchen walls. She threw a full straight. The next roll was better yet.

"Yahtzee!" she yelled, excited for a couple seconds.

He rolled without saying anything. Ended up putting seventeen in chance.

She won three rolls later.

"Call it a night?"

"Not yet."

ULTIMATE REALITY

He was damn good at hacky sack. He played on the side of the road, tall trees looming behind him as his leg kicked in all usable degrees within its lanky orbit.

It never dropped.

She looked from the backseat at his bare smile and saw it all.

ON THE CLOCK

The trail led through gnarled trees, leaning windswept trunks with skeletal branches, to the glimmering sea. The horizon lonely but infinite.

He sat inside a squat kiosk at the trailhead, cloistered from the unmistakably salty air, leafing slowly through a National Geographic, beholding the world's beauty.

BODY HEAT

Soft sun warmth yielded to the sea breeze chill. Gulls called overhead, and families laughed down shore.

They lay together, bodies clammy from swimming. She touched her stomach, he kissed her forehead.

Her head rolled gently over his chest. They held tighter, breeze blowing harder, tide crashes covering other sounds.

SUNRISE

They never went to sleep that night and walked barefoot onto the soccer field to watch the sun rise. After a night of talking, her sneezes were the only sound between them for a while.

"I love you."

"I love you, too."

Sometimes, like this, they said it.

THE WARRIOR

He spat into dirt and rubbed his fingers in it, creating muddy paste. He wiped a streak across his cheek. He spat again, did the other side.

He shut one eye, aimed his plastic bow, defeated the evildoer with a yellow arrow. Things would be better now. She'd see.

THE SHOW MUST GO ON

A bridge led from one side of the wash to the other, and the children ran across it dragging sticks against its metal-grated sides. One boy tripped, fell, dropped his stick. The others kept running. When he got up they had already crossed, like nothing had happened.

WORKING CLASS HERO

He went door-to-door selling wrapping paper for the school fundraiser. He wanted to be the top seller so he could win the Disneyland tickets. He went out for hours at a time, into the purpling dusk and past it.

He did not win the tickets in the end.

ACROSS THE STREET

Every night the garage light goes on at the neighbor's house. A couple lives there. Been married for a while, I think.

It turns on late, around ten. It goes off around two or three in the morning. I see it from my home office, long after the workday is done.

ROVER

He snuck out for a smoke at his parents' house. It was around two in the morning. The moon was yellow, full. The stray dog he picked up trotted around the backyard, wet nose in cold grass.

They loved the dog already. He was a good boy.

He needed that.

STORAGE

He looked through Polaroid pictures in a box. Old friends. Did they still listen to Radiohead?

He pulled through other remnants from a younger (past?) life, notebooks full of abstractions and doodles, burned CDs.

His stuff lay in printer paper boxes in his parents' garage, their junk surrounding it.

THE PEOPLE ONE HOUSE OVER

A siren sounded, normally distant. She thought nothing of it at first, but the shrill grew louder.

It crescendoed, then ended abruptly. She watched out the window. Soon he was on the stretcher. Blanket contours. Feet. Nose.

It struck her she did not know his name.

Or his wife's.

DISAPPEARING ACT

She told him she never knew he was at the party, which could have hurt but it did not bother him.

The truth was he barely remembered any of it, only that he wanted to leave as soon as he arrived. Probably no one else noticed, either. Hopefully so.

PAST ACQUAINTANCE

Stalled air loitered in the office lobby. It never went away. Ferns drooped. The elevator dinged timidly. People walked in gray strides, sharing neutral exchanges.

One day, a man ran through naked before being tackled by security. They all thought they knew him, but no one could say from where.

GAMES WE PLAY

She slept softly at his side, undisturbed from his waking. The workday was a few hours away.

He opened the front door gently and stepped onto the deck. He picked out gravel pebbles from the potted succulents, throwing them into the nearby field. The pots would need new gravel soon.

GAMES OF CHANCE

She played the casino's ATM like another one of the machines. She flipped through different accounts, tried her hand at each withdraw option, fingers dancing across the screen. Maybe this time it would hit.

Neither card was a winner. She finally walked away, though not towards the exit.

RAZOR'S EDGE

The metal was always cold when she pressed it against her gooseflesh skin. She tasted its precise edge through tactile sensation. An exquisite chill pricked through the lines she traced, memories gathering like constellations, vague representations, then receded as forgotten dreams.

Downstairs a kettle whistled. She shut her eyes.

A FIST THROUGH THE WINDOW

It started when her ex showed up unannounced, and her cousin said, "Only she would have two boyfriends come for Thanksgiving."

They didn't talk much, the three of them. She was supposed to come over later to his parents' house, he being her current boyfriend. But she didn't.

THE LOCAL MONSTER

The boy threw a rock through the window. The exquisite sound of breaking glass, like something collapsing under its own frail weight.

The boy set the shed afire. He watched flames consume splintered wood and spit out ash.

The boy defied the sign, learned what lived on the other side.

A QUICK BREAK

The boy had dirt on his face, ran through the tall grass into the trees. The others were somewhere behind him, yelling, throwing rocks. He looked through the bushes he hid in, saw two of them near, but looking in opposite directions. He sucked his thumb, safe for now.

ROAD STOP

She stopped for a beer. Her hair was down, her bike outside where it might stay. This was a good beer, and she had been riding a while.

They had rooms so she checked in. A coastal motel, every room an ocean view.

At night everything disappeared.

GLOSS

She smoked by the lake. She heard crying behind her, somewhere from one of the campsites. It had a stretched sound, a distorted timbre. It carried a rich sadness, a hiccoughing, stuttering pitch.

It had been a long time since she cried, remembered crying, though her eyes were always red.

LIFE IS SHORT

It was St. Patrick's Day and they went to a local Irish pub, but during the day, before all the assholes showed up.

Then the bagpipe band marched in, practically breaking glass. Bagpipes are particularly loud in small venues.

He covered his ears, waiting for it to end.

BUZZ KILL

They got stoned and watched a ventriloquist. It was wildly entertaining. The dummy was like a little person!

He was also an uptight dick. He reminded them of someone they knew who had no chill and called the cops on them once.

The show ended up being a real bummer.

WATCH HIM LIVE

The chimpanzee casually ate watermelon. He held the gnawed rind and swung on a hanging rope without warning or apparent purpose. He landed, chewed more, gripped the bars. He looked out at them, then swung on the rope again.

His caretakers took videos, notes. They said he was very smart.

PLEASANTRIES

He flicked paper clips at his desk. He tried to make them into the cup. He made some, missed some. The air conditioning was cold and buzzing.

She walked up unexpectedly, as people do at work, to ask him about an invoice.

He studied it, then, "Pending."

She thanked him.

ASSIGNMENT

She put her feet up on the table and watched another movie. How many had she seen now in this cramped room? Its mauve drapes and faded floral comforter. Photographic prints of endless plains, cattle herds. Another frigid morning at a barren site looming. She went to school for this.

UP FOR AIR

She woke early, head hurting, creases on her face from sleeping on the couch.

The living room was stuffy, thick with dust and dander. The dog asleep, supine. Her dad snoring in his hospital bed, feet on the ground for pain relief.

She lay still, but the day kept coming.

THE DRIVER

She drove in stops and starts. The starts were short-lived. The stops were abrupt, jerky.

Her mother breathed out, in fumes, gripping the door handle.

"Just be natural. You're bringing attention to us."

She tried, but kept braking. The cars were fast, honking. Her feet barely touched the pedals.

CLOSE CALL

116 degrees. He leaned back, yawned, tasted the hot air. A fly struggled in a spiderweb underneath the vending machine.

A car drove up, swerved, nearly crashed into a pump, then kept going.

Hand on chest, he exhaled. Then the fly broke free. He had never seen anything like it.

HONEST WORK

He spun a sign to advertise a lot of new homes recently built. It was honest work. No one got hurt.

Although all that spinning could hurt his wrists, and the standing was hard on the knees. Plus hot days were very hot and made him feel lightheaded.

CARRY ON

They laughed behind him as he walked, one leg several inches shorter than the other. He was new here, as he had been before, and this latest family venture the same as any other and the town beyond history with its movie theatre, shopping centers, and schools like these.

A SUNDAY MORNING FAR AWAY

She parked her truck with its wooden camper shell, AKA the bedroom, in a bank parking lot and called her friend. She smoked a joint, relaying everything: the money, his lawyer, her summons.

Her sunburnt forehead against the wheel, eyes squeezed shut.

"Yes," faintly. She was coming home.

THE MORNING

He couldn't find his toolbox at first, but eventually saw it behind some paint buckets. He looked around the garage, seeing nothing was in any kind of order.

He didn't know what he was going to make yet. He imagined a shelf or something useful. He had the time now.

THE CAMP

Morning. Shadows shifting glacially against the rock face beyond his camp. The wind breaking against his jacket, whipping his tarp. The fire burning, a crackle like footsteps over broken earth.

A couple passed. They looked at him but he did not return their attention.

Each day farther, closer, to home.

BONFIRE

Tall flames tangled against the starless midnight sky. Bodies dancing, arms on waists, heads on shoulders. Pops and hisses, howls and hollers. Sand in toes, fragments of ridged seashells alluringly sharp against their soles. They kept adding wood, in celebration of the end. No words spoke of the new beginning.

NOW BEFORE NEVER

They stood on the deck to watch the first visible flames knife over the mountaintop.

Mandatory evacuation in effect. If they stayed, they would be intruders in their own home.

They watched the fire steadily eat the hillside, draw nearer to the road. Over there, still, while they could.

WAIT FOR IT

She did not want to look. She went ahead and did the dishes, swept the floors. She thought about it, but painted her nails. Polka-dotted. She played on her phone while they dried.

She walked the dog because he kept looking at her.

He trotted, tail high, no hesitation.

BORED SICK

He was bored in the botanical gardens and their endless spring. She was taking pictures on her phone. He was on his phone too, thumbing through a catalogue of visual mindlessness: Fail videos, dank memes, creepy pastas.

The images were an escape, another world. Life could be dull.

TAI CHI ON THE BEACH

They turned their hips and twisted their heels into the sand. They held the world in soft hands, cupped it by the poles and dragged it across their hearts.

Surfers walked by, languid, overly upright. Maybe nursing wipeouts.

Their kids surfed.

They turned again. Crashing waves met their gaze.

SAFETY

She slid fast against the rain-soaked turf, flakes of itchy grass crawling onto her leading leg. Her foot struck the ball first, sent it upfield towards relative safety.

The opposing player stood now, shed her allegiance temporarily to ask if she was okay. The whistle sounded, so high-pitched.

THE VICTOR AND THE SPOILS

He won.

In the morning his lip was fatter, eye puffier. The ringing had settled, left the world blanketed in a familiar obfuscation.

The eggs were not cooking. He learned he never turned on the heat.

He burned them, rubbery yellow things. He wasn't hungry, anyway.

APPRENTICE

The boy was in trouble again. The hot whip of the belt left a cold, searing imprint. Its temperature inhaled and exhaled with him.

He ate his beatings like a meal, noticed the subtleties, learned the nuances.

It went on this way, until he knew just where to strike.

STRIKE

He swung and missed. He put his head down, but caught himself before spending too long at the plate. He walked quickly to the dugout.

They were winning, and ultimately did win, but that didn't matter.

The voice behind him, silent. The verdict ahead of him, settled. As always.

THE TELL

The tunnel was a concrete theatre to graffiti and litter. Broken bottles, crinkled cans. Cellophane.

The boys walked over garbage, traced the cold, paint-slick walls with their fingertips.

One revealed cigarettes. They lit up, coughed, watched the smoke dance.

One puked. They laughed.

At home, he told his parents.

GROCERY SHOPPING

They were allowed to roll the grocery cart home, to what was still their house.

He was missing something, and went back out into the night. When he returned, she asked if he found it.

"Yeah, I found it," he said, tossing the run-over watch face onto the table.

SCHRÖDINGER'S CAT

He dug through the outside trash but found nothing. He shook worse now. The sun was out but an unremitting coldness iced through him.

He poured the can over, rummaged through, cut his hand on broken glass. Did it break just now? The despair of impossible knowledge was almost worse.

ENOUGH TO

He put his phone down, the news was enough.

Enough? Too little? Too much?

Maybe enough. He did not know what.

He went to the deck to get fresh air, cool against his perspiry forehead.

He unclenched the railing, knuckles white, watched color return, as though it meant something.

THE MALL'S GETTING A HIP BOWLING ALLEY, TOO

They had everything they needed. The apartment complex had restaurants, a gym, and a killer coffee shop. The mall next door had a movie theatre.

Best of all was that their office was down the street. Of course, the WiFi was so good they could work anywhere when necessary.

THE SMELL OF PAINT

He walked in first, flicked on the light in the living room, casting a yellow pall. It was smaller than they remembered. The kitchen, too.

He opened the plastic blinds, thin, dusty. Constant streams of traffic.

They held each other, quietly rocking, boxes still in the car.

IT WOULD BE SO GOOD

His shirt half-tucked, his pants too long, his ancient shoes worn to a smudged gray. White, thin hair a disheveled flop.

"Can I have some popcorn, please?" he asked again over the counter.

He craned his neck over, searching. No one came.

SALT

She cracked the egg that was left and fried it.

A fried egg was better than a scrambled egg. Two distinct parts, like two courses.

She broke the yolk. She hated broken yolks.

She threw the spatula, screaming. It would be three days until she could buy eggs again.

A GOOD DAY

It was hard to feel after such a normal day. Maybe it was a good day. He made his coworkers laugh during the staff meeting. It was a lively icebreaker.

At home he stared at the animal hospital across the street. A busy night with a lot full of cars.

THE TRUTH WILL SET YOU FREE

He put his hand to his face and ducked out of the way from the phone. The couple huddled close, pretending to take a selfie, but he knew they were really taking a picture of him.

Informants lined the streets. Cameras on streetlights, microphones in bushes. Vigilant, he continued, unafraid.

HOW HE SPENT HIS DAY

He started out quiet, but talked more as the day went on, making all kinds of new friends.

He started telling jokes several hours in, to some degree of laughter. He bought beers for strangers.

He left sometime when it was dark out, motioned at cars on the walk home.

THE PANEL

"Nate?" he asked.

"Nathan," he corrected.

He sat. Was the chair broken or something? It felt wobbly.

His first answer sounded like someone else said it. The next few gained coherence, but he mispronounced a couple words. They smiled nicely.

He thanked them each by name.

"Thank you, Nate."

SIDE CONVERSATIONS

She went to talk to him while they were still there. She and he could be seen talking near the kitchen sink. Neither were smiling. He rested his hand on the counter, looking at her as she spoke.

They found her after, on the front porch watching the rain.

CLASSIC ROCK

Eruption. A seismic, regrettable flash.

He sat alone in the garage in a foldout chair, low to the ground, asking himself the same question again, shaking.

Baking upstairs, she paused, dried her eyes. Time, invitations, cupcakes - up in the air.

Outside, music from the neighboring car lot. Saturday. Activity everywhere.

CLEAN LAUNDRY

She poured the basket of laundry over the bed, a soft, tumbling burst. Renewed fabrics striped in morning light.

She folded hand towels into neat squares, rolled an open palm over creases. Paired socks, hung shirts. A stray tee stopped her. She held it in both hands.

LIKE A NEW WORD

They had a good system for being somewhere else while the other packed.

He botched it one day, showed up early.

"Sorry."

Her eyes watered, she shook her head. He did too, his throat desert dry.

"Sorry," he repeated, feeling the word, his lips curl then flatten at the end.

GALE WIND IN A PAPER BAG

He put his hand over hers. Her mouth sucked closed, opened back up as the oxygen pushed through her.

The doctor used the term "quality of life." It had a compassionate, distant sound to it.

He watched the mechanism of breath charge forward uninterrupted. She lied there through it all.

LAST NIGHT AT THE RED DOOR

It was a busy night at the tavern. Smoke, booze everywhere. Jukebox rock music. Laughter among men, women. Dancing.

They were there. He grabbed him, she yelled. He threw him down on the pool table and stuck the knife in his throat.

He watched her embrace him one last time.

A KIND OF FREEDOM

Cracked charcoal patterns, spiderwebs and feather bunches, spread as far as could be seen across the exploded sky. Far below, through the thick, gunmetal air, the horse ran, its bulging legs driving, white chest heaving, and mane flowing as coral waves undersea. No other living thing around for miles.

BUT WHAT WAS IT LIKE?

For all the volumes written in history and of it, pages turned soundless for how long? Language spoken at the first flame's hiss, the heave of a pyramid brick, a staff thud against castle floor, hysteria at a village plundered, an oar dipping into virgin waters of the Willamette - lost.

I AM

Something happened.

The synths turned milky, slogged against the amphetamine drum pulse. The vibration rode up her legs and into her chest. Dancing happened through her, electric, automatic.

The color. The light. Everything was easy.

He was gone.

She let go, gave in, saw through it all.

She was gone.

BIG PICTURE

He scanned the sky for constellations he could recognize. It was hard on a night so littered with heavenly bodies, in a place so far from city lights and traffic.

He thought he would pick out many, but realized how little he knew.

MIND OFF

He washed dishes, mopped the floor, wiped the stove clean. A stubborn spot needed extra scrubbing. Almost all of it came out, or at least it was fainter now.

Time well spent.

Time doing.

Time fighting.

RESONATE

"Baby," she said. "Do you like my tits like this?" She spread her breasts apart, exaggerated. "Or like this?" She pushed them together, making cleavage.

"Oh baby."

She put the pillows together, closing the gap.

"Pillows are the tits of the bed."

He never made the bed improperly again.

THE REPORT FROM UTOPIA

His friend was in town from way up north. They kicked a soccer ball around in the park, shared news.

His friend had plenty. Things were happening. People were alive. Culture. Art. Food.

Sex. A healthy, human appetite and appreciation.

Everywhere.

They had beer after, time for part two.

A CONVERSATION WHILE WAITING FOR THE BALL TO DROP

They argued politics, one speaking louder than the other, if it could really be called speaking. Others were around, so they went outside.

The louder one did not smoke, but accepted the cigarette.

They reached their idealogical differences, made plain their disagreement.

The cold bit, completely itself, pure and true.

A BIG DEAL

Apparently it was Boss' Day. He stopped paying attention to that after the first year. To him it was like International Men's Day or something.

His coworker gave their boss a card, handed it over right in front of him. He waited until the meeting continued, requested spreadsheets in hand.

BREAK

The wall in the break room was terra cotta orange. The window was gridded with metal dividers and flimsy black blinds. HR posters detailing workplace rights, notices, covered the bulletin boards.

His worst poems were written in that room. His dullest material thudded, a rubber mallet of inspiration.

SLEEPOVER

They watched internet videos hours into the night. They learned about laser systems used in Atlantis, ancient structures visible on Mars, and secret world orders. The world was magical, but dangerous, full of lies and corruption. Why couldn't people wake up?

Tired, but unstoppable, they played the next.

STEALING FROM DOGS

A tennis ball was on the front lawn. Its ratty fuzz a muddy yellow, darkened and matted. It was missing altogether in some places, rubber the color of prosthetic limbs bare and sad.

He picked it up as he walked by, a new treasure.

CHOICE

She counted change from her car in the parking lot, fingers hunting through plastic wrappers and wrinkled receipts. The cup holders were sticky with something.

She had enough for a slushee, thankfully.

She teared up, feeling ridiculous, then got to business with the choice at hand.

Red or blue?

SHED

She cut her hair short. The tops of her ears showed now. She looked at them in the mirror, absorbing their visibility.

Walking, the air felt colder, but richer. It moved in layers, revealed undulating textures that before were hidden to her.

This is what it felt like, letting go.

MOVE ON

She ran beside the river for miles. Its green-hued water rippled yellow in the morning. Others were around, always were, but were bubbles floating, bursting, disappearing. Every step made perfectly alone.

This place, dirty and pure, always gave her what she gave it. Each breath an investment in tomorrow.

PRETENDING

Seven months in and it's still hard making friends. People move slower with more space between them.

I walked outside after they left. She stayed inside, quiet, reading already.

The moon, orange and low, half-obscured by treetop silhouettes. Pretending to be full, pretending to be a perfect circle.

WAITING

Bras and panties laid like produce in crates in the lingerie store.

He imagined the mannequin busts and asses were specially crafted for effect. He looked at them while she tried on bras in the fitting room.

Wait, did someone see that? It wasn't like that.

AN UNDERSTANDING FROM THIN AIR

The magician worked the room. Everyone was having a good time. Alcohol and card tricks make a good team.

One sullen guest sneered at the ten of hearts.

"Yeah, it's my card. None of this matters anyway. Life is pointless."

The magician nodded thoughtfully, eyes sincere. It astonished him.

WHERE'D YOU GET THOSE?

She walked past the bed in a thin slip. He was sick but she made him forget that, even as he hacked phlegm and shook from chills running down his legs.

"What should I wear when you get sick?"

She tossed a pair of small shorts onto his hot face.

OH

She danced with him because she wanted to dance and he was out there with the music playing and the older people moving around the floor.

When she was done she walked smiling to a table and kissed another man.

He kept dancing, as though hiding.

UNDERWATER CABBAGE IS HAPPY

She drew an octopus. It had a bulbous body/head. The innermost legs were thin and curled up around the body/head. It had a red smile.

Another low art grade. According to her teacher, it lacked proportion. Also, octopuses are not purple.

She must have liked the smile, though.

GO GET 'EM, TIGER

The floor was splattered in orange. Then she saw the boy, painted in stripes.

"I want to be a tiger," he said.

She took a picture, then washed him.

"But I want to be a tiger."

She put a raw steak before him at dinner.

"I'll be a boy."

BACK TO THE DRAWING BOARD

Everything he wrote felt close to good, but was off by a few words. The poems lacked punch. They were complete, beyond partial sketches. They worked, just not optimally.

He pounded out a journal entry-type thing, effortlessly, capturing all he felt.

But that was too easy.

WHY DO YOU?

She made thousands of clay figures. A garden littered with fantastic life. Lily pads with eyes. Frogs with teeth. Two-headed harpists playing to aristocrat rabbits, go-go dancer wolves in cages around them.

People asked her why she made them. Defining their purpose the most fantastic pursuit of all.

AWAY FOR THE SUMMER

The children ran wild off the pier into the lake, green with murk. Trees surrounded them as they splashed and populated the day with their laughter.

She cleaned the rowboat onshore, as told. Days here were getting easier, watching the sunlight ripple again.

ANEW

It rained so they cancelled going to the beach. It was their only day off that week.

After sitting there for an hour on their phones she had enough.

"Let's go."

So funny, they thought, that they had only used this oversized, rainbow umbrella to fend off the sun.

THE DANCE

"I really like you."

"I really like you, too."

"I enjoy spending time with you."

"You're so fun to be with."

"I care about you."

"You mean a lot to me."

Soon.

FLING

He sat alone at the pool with his feet in the water. Everyone else was inside.

She walked over. They had seen each other around. They talked, drank beer. When it was right, they kissed.

Soon after, her dad switched jobs. The family moved. Their first time their last goodbye.

WITNESS

They came at night, danced barefoot, worshipers at the altar. The trees and cactuses stood immeasurably stoic, possessing undeniable authority.

They heard them speak, subtle whispers through breeze-blown leaves and moon-illumined spines. A felt wisdom, a call to quiet. A rejection of childish thoughts.

PROMISING OPPORTUNITIES

An expansive, mid-century house in the hills was renting for $4,000 a month.

"We could get 20 of us together. People do that."

He called the realtor.

"Yes, please call me back. We're very interested."

$200 a month was doable for any working 18 year-old.

LIFT UP YOUR VOICE

He sang songs all night until his voice was hoarse and ragged. Other places hurt worse in the morning, but it was worth it.

He shuffled to the kitchen, joints creaking, and stared off outside. The white sun looked lonely.

He sang once more, a spontaneous stream, a baritone gurgle.

REFUGE

She wiggled in the grass, magnifying glass to her eye, the yelling distant now. Ladybugs wobbled on stalks and leaves, the breeze brushing over them. When the wind picked up, it toppled a couple over, but they fluttered their spotted wings and flew to somewhere more stable, easily enough.

SANCTUARY

She sat in the back while they argued up front. Endless grievances. Misplaced items, undone chores. Lies, anger. Broken moments never fixed.

She beat them out the car by a mile. The air stunk from industry. The rest stop filthy.

She stayed in the stall as long as she could.

MARINE LAYER

She always cleaned the bathrooms first so she could look out the windows as she worked on the dining rooms. She moved slower than usual this morning, extra sore from her graveyard shift at the distribution center. So did the sun, at least it seemed, as though just for her.

SIGHTSEEING

They sat close on the subway. It was crowded, many people standing. Mundane but exciting. They had never been to the city.

They got off at the wrong stop, but agreed it was nice to walk.

It happened fast, her purse gone, like a cruel satire starring them.

INNOCENCE LOST

She took the red candy because red always tasted best. Then it got weird, revealed a metallic taste and stinging heat. It tickled her throat.

She told her mom, who said it must be hot cinnamon.

"I don't like cimmamum."

Red candy was never the same.

STAND ANYWHERE BUT STILL

They had not spoken in a while and he did not know what she was doing now. The space helped, but it wasn't everything.

He started volunteering at a food bank. Loaded bags with dry goods, gave them to people lined up to receive them. His smiles large, forced.

WANTED: CANDY CANE DANCER, F/T, BENEFITS, PTO/PATERNITY LEAVE

He was paid $200 to dress as a candy cane and dance for three hours at a magazine's holiday party. The magazine was dedicated to pot so the organizers also gave him a potent cookie to eat.

If all jobs were like this, then everyday would be Christmas.

IN/OUT

He rode his skateboard down into the bowl, lifted onto the lip, grinded down his trucks, hovering between in and out, and swooped back into the bowl.

He took for granted that it took work to make it feel so easy. His only ambition was to play his whole life.

PATIENT ZERO

The squirrel chattered, tail agitated.

She stopped and imitated it. He kept walking.

"Why do you hate squirrels?"

"One day one of them is going to bite you."

"Then I'll get the squirrel disease and give it to you!"

"We'll start the zombie apocalypse, you and me, baby."

FRAME OF SOUND

He drove home fast, music blaring. He never particularly liked this album, but he did not know what he wanted to hear and he liked the first song.

This loud, on this night, it had new life. The bass throbbed. A violent ocean, a building collapsing. The end at last.

GO AHEAD

They sat waiting on the boardwalk for the photo booth. The seaside air smelled like hot dogs and people. He ran the balloon over her hair, strands springing up like seaweed reaching. She jerked to bite his nose but licked it instead. They made it in eventually, their hair wild.

CLEAR EYES

She woke on her own. The early summer sky was soft blue ahead of her alarm.

There was no headache this morning. There were no bad dreams during the night.

She opened a window, leaned out, soaked in sun.

It was like a dream, but a good one.

ALIAS

Sometimes people asked her why she was alone or where she was going. Sometimes people asked her name. Sometimes they told her to smile.

She made up stories now. To get mad would be unbecoming for Genevieve Hightower, Martian biologist. People were amazed they had never heard of her.

REAL FRIENDS TELL THE TRUTH

The urinal pad read, "Say no to drugs."

He wondered, pissing on it, if this particular PSA had ever resonated with anyone, anywhere.

Was it a turning point? Did someone attend a meeting, check in, say the urinal sent him?

"That old bastard. Tell him I said hello."

SEND A MESSAGE

He scribbled on the sign in black marker. A squiggle of defiance over the call to obedience. Clotted the message, attacked its passage to future eyes.

NO SPITTING

He did not spit, however, on the sign or near it.

TEACH WHAT YOU KNOW

It was impossible to say what started it. An undermining joke from the back row. A crude noise elsewhere. Jarring commotion from a phone, its volume brazenly high.

He dropped the marker, mounted the desk, screamed at the top of his lungs. Among them, of them, his final lecture.

JUST BE NICE TO ME PLEASE

He never quite yelled. It was more like passionate muttering.

He paced back and forth on the sidewalk, naked as a baby with arms flailing, sputtering gibberish.

"Stop yelling at me," he told himself.

The authorities were firm, but calm, as they placed him in the back of the car.

IT DOESN'T GET EASIER

Two old men played chess over a stool, flies and humidity surrounding them. The one in suspenders moved his rook, lost it to a knight. He brought his queen into play and took the knight.

"I didn't see that coming," his friend said.

"Imagine how many times you've said that?"

BETTER THAN LISTENING TO THE DUDE FROM HR TALK ABOUT THE WEATHER

He played loud, fast, whipped his sweaty hair back but some strands fell over his eyes, which were closed as he sang.

Ten or so people watched his band play. Two took the CD, which was free. It was Monday, and he had had many, many, worse than this.

PRIMER FOR THE SHOW

He wore a plastic Halloween skeleton mask to school every day. His teacher always made him take it off, which he did, with less resistance than he used to give. He understood it was against the rules but he needed to be himself.

He wore it all recess-long, always.

CAN'T MASK RELIEF

She sucked a lemon wedge, rubbed the rind in her hands, fervently washing the smell of smoke from her fingers.

"Hello!" she said entering, kissing her grand-mother on the cheek.

"I didn't see you in the backyard, sweetie."

"Me neither," her mom said.

"Here I am!" arms outstretched.

SIGN OF LIFE

Her neighbor's husband died. She knocked on the door. No answer. The house was two stories, she might not have heard it.

She took out the trash that night, tiptoed to peek into the backyard. A blue glow against the white fence. Dull, then bright, then dull again.

MOVING PICTURES

The TV was muted. It helped her sleep. Old sit-coms blared without laugh tracks. The looks on their faces. Someone was in trouble...

A phone sex commercial appeared. Soft focus. Pink boas. Blondes in front of sequined curtains.

She was brunette now, gratefully had meaningful work. Still an insomniac, though.

AT HOME IN THE WINTER

It was quite cold out and star-shaped patterns frosted the windows. She had only a windbreaker but it would be just a cigarette's worth of exposure.

She spied them talking inside, animated and standing close. She smoked another, the cold a quiet confidante.

FAILURE FLAG

He painted the newest toy soldiers yellow, except for their helmets, which he made white. They were going to be an army of retreat. He needed cowards. His battlefield, its corn starch trenches and painted-on creeks, had too many heroes. His fantasy world needed reality, someone to blow it.

COACH

The coach ran laps around the field before practice. Cut grass, fresh air. His lungs primed to yell, to awaken.

He pounded Gatorade, pissed at his secret spot behind the weight room.

When the team arrived, he began practice by quoting Vince Lombardi.

They lost again Friday, but by less.

SHOULD'VE AIMED HIGHER

The Ferris Wheel flashed red and lilac like a valentine love letter. Sweet, batter-rich, food smells consumed the air at ground level. A stuffed monkey she won poked its head from her purse. If he'd won it for her would she have kissed him back, way up there?

MOUTHFUL OF FLOWERS

The theatre lights dimmed. Now what? She sat there so still with her long, thin arms over the armrests.

He turned his face several times without leaning over until they both did and kissed slowly, strangely, as though learning how to speak.

It was senseless, but they understood.

CEREMONY

She finished sewing her dress the night before her wedding. She hung it and looked at it for a while.

He worked delicately on his beard, trimming hairs with scissors. He preferred that to an electric shaver, its conforming consistency.

They slept separately that night, holding out and holding on.

ZZZ

All they wanted was to be alone. The keycard was stubborn, unforgiving, but at last the door gave way. She slumped to the closest bed and managed her shirt off over wet hair. He leaned against the wall watching her, slid down slowly to his heels, gently shutting his eyes.

GO FISH

"Baby there's a fish in the sky. Come look."

"Baby, what are you talking about there's a fish in the sky?"

"In the clouds. Thin, elongated strata or whatever. Has the mouth, eye, dorsal fin."

"Then it's a cloud. Don't sound so crazy! And dorsal fin?"

WAIT!

He ran out after her car, arms flailing. She saw him, an ostrich in flight. She braked until he almost caught up, then drove off again.

He saw her eyes in the rearview mirror, knew the smile beneath them.

She stopped. Red, he admitted it wasn't that important after all.

NOT THERE YET

They jostled together on the seat, legs dangling, knees knocking.

"Give it back!"

Nothing was given.

"Stop it!"

Nothing was stopped.

"Owww!"

The car braked and the talk came.

Something was given, something else was stopped.

Peace followed, until a slug bug passed them.

All was taken, all was stopped.

YES THEY CAN!

She looked obsessively at the toad, opened up its tank, grazed its bumpy body with her fingertips until she felt brave enough to pick it up and hold it.

One day after school it was gone. Her dad told her it ran away, which she believed for many years.

SEE WHAT HAPPENS

An artificial lagoon sat green and sad looking, reflecting like neon algae in sunlight. Caged animals lined the dirt loop around it. Birds and lizards. Then a monkey, a camel, even a baby giraffe. Maybe it was for the worst, but she undid the latch. It was within arm's reach.

CELEBRATION

She moved with magical speed, a transfixing slowness, as she twisted over and bare against the cold sheets. He followed, walked forward and over her on hands and knees. They teased, took their time, or tried. They were too eager. It was a fun night.

The dog, his birthday, slept.

LOVE THE ONE YOU'RE WITH

The apple cactus grew quickly by the living room window. It was stocky, singular in its vertical direction. Spiny white knobs broke free on top, soon giving bloom to star-shaped growths. Soft yellows faded into green.

They named it Yuri. They had wanted a dog but were never home.

ALL YOU HAVE

It went to someone else.

So it would not be over yet. And tomorrow she would be back, again, ad infinitum.

On her break she walked, reminded her posture not to slump. Passing the begonias, she placed her mind on the soft sunlight squeezing through their thin, papery petals.

CHARITY

He walked up to a box of food at the doorstep. Canned goods, protein bars, and bags colored red, white, and blue.

He sat outside eating peanuts, savory and comforting, tossing dirty-feeling shells at the mostly dirt yard.

The house was foreclosed for everyone to see.

PERIPHERAL SHELVES

Students mostly used the school library for its computers. The uncommon occasion when someone checked out a book was a pleasant jolt for the librarian. She opened the inside cover, stamped it, noting the last check-out date, savoring the smell of old, forgotten paper waking after a long rest.

ONE FOR THE ROAD

The pornography lady, as the hospice volunteer later called her, selected the pages from the book to be read to her.

After the volunteer read the word 'penis' aloud for the third time, she asked, blushing, "Is this uncomfortable for you?"

"No. But I can tell it is for you."

GETTING OLDER AGAIN

As a strange joke, she bought her friend a human skull for a birthday gift. She also gave her makeup, to be nice.

When her friend opened her gifts, the next step was obvious. She had little makeup left by the end of it, and the skull had a name.

PERFECT SENSE

The knoll was dew-kissed in the predawn. The ice block was plenty, but the condensation enlivened their course. They giggled, swore it would be faster.

They took turns whizzing down into the brightening morning, until the ice melted beyond use. They each licked it, a spontaneous, meaningful goodbye.

TEAMWORK

He saw the bus approaching, early again. He took off sprinting, the hot day made hotter by his black jeans blurring space and time.

He made it, barely, sweating and dizzy. He tripped boarding, then a breathless woman eked in behind him. The doors grunted closed before either could sit.

HOLD THE ROOF AS PILLARS AND THE SPACES IN BETWEEN

The doves flew into the yard again. They pecked the dirt, heads dipping and bobbing, feet stuttering. They flapped their wings, lifted off, paper fans opening. They flew in separate directions. The larger one landed on a telephone wire, the smaller in a tree. They would be back, together again.

PHILOSOPHER STUMP

The hill was undeveloped and unfettered by the cares of who sat on it. A smiling plot of weeds and wildflowers, and a fell tree to sit on and consider the world.

They sat quiet, chins on fists, piecing together what remained of what wasn't said.

SITTING

The terminal seemed busy for a Wednesday, but he never travelled much, so what did he know?

He sat cross-legged, hands in a mudra, eyes shut, and smiling. No one paid attention to him. They all were doing something similar, in their own way. All just passing the time.

LET GO

The balloon floated away from her. He lifted her as she cried. She reached her hand up, as though she was close enough to grab it now.

He rocked her, said to enjoy watching it, a red dot disappearing. Suddenly, it was like that was its purpose all along.

HEIRLOOM

He learned quilting from his grandmother. Her wrinkled hands fleshy waves crashing against mortal shores. Her effort perpetual.

This quilt, unfinished but close, was already years old. The silent question over its completion hovered, but was never spoken.

Their hands answered together, now and always.

BIRTHDAY CAKE

He brought her a birthday cake. He did not tell her he made it, not until she tried it.

He took her picture, her smile and the cake. She beamed, immediately precious.

The cake was dry, frosting too sweet.

"I made it."

She kissed him, beaming, forever rare.

FRIENDS

She stepped outside to listen to music, the moon wrapped in a gauzy haze. A bat swung in and out of visibility around a tree. Chaotic dips and swoops. It looked lost. This was the suburbs.

She turned the music louder. The Misfits. She imagined the bat feeling at home.

BIRDSEYE

She walked. Not to any particular place, that would be counterproductive. The point was simply to saunter, like Thoreau had talked about in 'Walking.'

She stopped at a freeway overpass, wrapped her fingers through its metal fencing, pulled herself forward to look down at endless cars underneath her feet.

HAT

He held his leather cowboy hat, ran a thumb around its brim.

A neighbor he did not know called him "Crocodile Dundee."

Of course, that neighbor he did not know lived in a house. He lived behind the dumpster across the road.

Everyday he walked. His hat on, head high.

COME WITH ME

How much French toast did the kitchen make? Its sweet smell filled the bathroom. Fantastic.

"Baby you have to."

"Baby I can't."

"They're gender neutral now. C'mon."

She was floored. They laughed, kissed. He lowered the lid and she straddled him, his face in her chest. Outstanding.

PRECEDENT

She opened the door. That was enough. He kissed her, ran his hands down her curves and pushed her onto the couch. She took his face, lips over lips, stubble, jaw and neck. He held tighter.

They were really late to the party. And would be many times again.

LATE TO THE PARTY

She thanked them over and over for coming, offered them drinks immediately. Cheese and other snacks spread on her little kitchen table, some balloons in the corner. One other person was there, on the couch.

Someone else came later. She kept calling it a party. They were glad they went.

NEW RELIGION

She started a dance church in the woods. She used an unoccupied store for service every Sunday. Devotees twisted, leapt, gyrated to whatever music played. Songs that opened or closed with rain sounds were prominent.

It became obvious. It became truth. God is motion. Every moment the big bang.

LULLABY JAM

The cymbals were no longer her default. She started playing the high-hat in concert with the bass drum. Young limbs blooming in autonomy. Her dad played his bass guitar beside her in the garage now, jamming together towards joyful exhaustion. Bedtimes came earlier, and without fuss. A natural rhythm.

FIVE STARS

The reviews for the motel were basically positive, though one stood out to her:

Bugs crawled on me in the bed where I slept at night.

Phenomenal. Did she not realize her meter? How simply she captured such unsettling environs?

She booked a room to experience it for herself.

MIRROR

He typed like he was playing the piano. He listened to music he enjoyed, wrote whatever came to mind without stopping. A spontaneous exercise without any goal in mind. A straight line. A zigzag. Something on the screen and off his chest.

He read it back, then revised it.

RUSH ORDER

He tore a ticket off the wire, strung clips jangling. A squat, horizontal window framed the bodies outside the truck. Another of endless orders.

The child dropped her cheesy tater tots immediately as she received them. He worked that much faster, she stopped crying that much sooner.

HOW THE TADPOLES HURRY

His dad took him frog catching. Croaks a chorus as daylight slipped away from the creek, a pink sun descending.

Mud sloshed underfoot, water squeezed between his toes. His velcro shoes thin protection.

The tadpoles were mesmerizing. Frenzied action in small spaces.

He never left empty-handed.

HARVEST MOON

They pulled over to sleep off the dirt road. The harvest moon low, large, orange. They lay in the back under a sleeping bag fully unzipped. Owls hooted. Crickets chirped. All else was stillness. Closely, they swore they heard strumming, a mystery ballad about moments never known again.

THANKS

He did not talk but always smiled. His pony-tailed hair shining black, hands huge. As the country club's janitor, rooms conformed to his presence.

The servers called him Chief Broom. They saved food from wedding receptions for him. His kindness, eyes full, his thanks.

FUND

The bottles were full of change and paper money. Everyone must have contributed. It was a small town, but felt larger lately.

The bottles were on counters at the deli, grocery store, gas stations, and schools. Tam's also had one.

People smiled at each other. Town felt smaller lately, too.

THE FINAL STANZA

He was a homeless poet and locals knew him. He exchanged his poems for spare change. He did not go hungry.

His poetry was observational. Children playing, people arguing, reasons for living during rainy weather.

When he died, people read their personal favorites of his across sunlit pages.

EARTHLINGS

Planes of hot, white light cascaded down from little conical fixtures evenly spaced throughout the gallery. Illuminated abstractions, zealous color, geometric landscapes floating in space.

She looked at another squiggled line, saying, "Imagine an alien anthropologist trying to decipher the human experience through something like this?"

He kissed her cheek.

BENDS TOWARDS MAGIC

The tree was a bearer of stories. Remembered, imagined. Sometimes both.

Its branches meandering, reaching, transforming. Sunlight bends towards magic. A hydra's sprouted necks. A woman's form twisted in dance. A crucifix. Two bodies embracing for all time.

They lay underneath it, filtered sunlight falling on their faces, to rest.

CATHEDRAL

They drove through farmlands, golden rolling hills and cows standing in place, a tractor parked on sloping earth, bowing trees bedraggled by time.

They stopped at a vista. They held hands first, then looked into each other's eyes.

Standing together, all spoke in silence. They were going to be okay.

HORIZON

Her arms over his shoulders, fingers rubbing into his back, into him. He held fixed around her waist. Their hips rocked together, drumbeats pulling, cymbals splashing.

It was a crowded room but they were infinitely alone, and acutely aware the music was finite. They kept dancing, one for the other.

Each of the 200 stories collected here are written in 50 words or fewer. The word limit is strict and without loopholes. Contractions count as two words. Acronyms count for as many words as the letters represented. For example, "CD" counts for two, "AKA" counts for three. Titles do not count against the word limit, though they are often integral to a story's plot and meaning.

Each story here is original, though a handful have appeared previously in similar or identical form in literary journals, each of which I'm happy to list here (whether they are defunct or still among the living):

Audience - *Twenty2o Journal*

The Camp - *Spartan*

It Would be so Good - *OneFortyFiction*

Underwater Cabbage is Happy - *Okay Donkey*

Sightseeing - *Blink Ink*

Real Friends Tell the Truth - *Misery Tourism*

Sign of Life - *The Citron Review*

ABOUT THE AUTHOR

Sean Pravica is a Californian writer and the author of *Stumbling Out the Stable*. He enjoys ample time outside with his partner, Danelze, with a special place in their hearts for the Mojave Desert and the Eastern Sierra.